ANDREW MATTHEWS

Wickedoz

Illustrated by Tony Ross

MAMMOTH

For Joanne, with love

First published in Great Britain 1990
by Methuen Children's Books Limited
Published 1991 by Mammoth
an imprint of Mandarin Paperbacks
Michelin House, 81 Fulham Road, London SW3 6RB
Reprinted 1992

Mandarin is an imprint of the Octopus Publishing Group,
a division of Reed International Books Limited

Text copyright © 1990 by Andrew Matthews
Illustrations copyright © 1990 by Tony Ross

ISBN 0 7497 0598 1

A CIP catalogue record for this title
is available from the British Library

Printed in Great Britain
by Cox & Wyman Ltd, Reading, Berks

CONTENTS

Chapter One: The Witch's Cat   7

Chapter Two: A Lot to Learn   13

Chapter Three: Living on Wits   19

Chapter Four: Snarl   24

Chapter Five: Bold Outlaws   32

Chapter Six: The Duke of Boldcombe   40

Chapter Seven: Mistress Moonwater
Rules OK   47

Chapter Eight: Wickedoz the Traitor   54

Chapter Nine: Spells and Shelves   60

Chapter Ten: Fortune   67

CHAPTER ONE

The Witch's Cat

Wickedoz was a witch's cat and he looked like a witch's cat ought to look. His coat was blacker than the inside of a coal mine at midnight. His eyes were the colour of runny honey and when he half-closed them when he was thinking, it made him look mysterious and magic. When Wickedoz moved, he was as slinky and silent as a blot of black ink wiggling down a page.

The witch who owned Wickedoz was called Tottie Gribble. She was a grubby sort of witch who lived in a filthy hovel half way up the side of a stony mountain. When Tottie was casting spells on her neighbours, to give them earache or bluebottles, she was happy. The rest of the time she was an ugly, cantankerous old hag.

One morning, Tottie returned from market

with a basketful of sweet-smelling herbs and a sour face. Wickedoz was curled up fast asleep on a pile of old rags, so he didn't see Tottie stumping about the hovel, nor did he hear what she was muttering to herself.

'If Farmer Pether thinks he can talk to me like that and get away with it, he's got a nasty shock coming!' she seethed. 'I'll give him warts! I'll give him spots! I'll give him goat pox!'

When Wickedoz woke a little later, Tottie was bent over a cauldron that was bubbling on the fire. She was adding various things to it from the pots, jars and flasks that were spread out on the table in front of her. Wickedoz yawned, stretched and knitted the rags with his claws. Tottie heard the scratching sound, looked up from her cauldron and glared.

'So!' she croaked, sprinkling bats' tongues into the pot. 'Awake at last, are you? I've never known a cat as lazy as you are! Lazy, cowardly and good for nothing! You're a waste of time and money! Tell me one good thing about you! Go on! Just one good thing!'

'W-e-l-l,' said Wickedoz, 'I'm outstandingly good-looking, you must admit. And I can talk, so I'm company for you in the evenings.'

'Company? Fiddlesticks!' snapped Tottie, slicing up a wyvern's nostril. 'I would have been better off with an adder, or a horned toad!'

'Ah, but they wouldn't have been as cuddly as I am!' purred Wickedoz.

'But you're not cuddly at all!' protested Tottie. 'Every time I try to cuddle you, you run a mile!'

'That's not my fault!' grumbled Wickedoz. 'You smell of magic all the time. I can't stand the smell of magic.'

'Well, of course I smell of magic!' screeched Tottie. 'I'm a witch, aren't I?' She was in such a temper that she dropped a filletted fenny-snake on the floor.

'Talking of smells,' said Wickedoz, 'I don't know what you're cooking in that pot, but it stinks! Haven't you got a bit of fish you could fry up?'

'This isn't lunch, you stupid animal!' growled Tottie. 'It's a spell I'm getting ready.'

'Ugh! Spells!' shuddered Wickedoz, frisking his tail. 'Don't even talk about them! I hate all that magic stuff! It's so scary!'

Tottie jumped up and down with annoyance. She made the table shake and the bottles on it rattled together.

'I do believe that there never was such an aggravating cat in the history of witchcraft!' she squealed, waving around a handful of mermaid's scales. 'All I want is a bit of peace and quiet so I can get on with a nice mean and nasty spell. But do I get it? Oh, no! My cat comes poking his big nose in and –'

'Er . . . watch out!' called Wickedoz.

The angrier Tottie became, the higher she bounced and she had worked herself up into such a rage that she was bouncing up higher

than a kangaroo on a trampoline.

'Mind the ceiling!' shouted Wickedoz.

It was too late. Tottie's head went – BONK! – against a black beam and she fell on to the table with a dreadful crash. Potions, powders, red and blue liquids, feathers, claws and mushrooms all mixed together and started to fizz. There was a loud explosion and a bright flash, followed by clouds of evil-smelling green smoke. When the smoke cleared, there was nothing left of Tottie Gribble but a sooty mark on the ceiling.

'I tried to warn her!' sighed Wickedoz. 'I kept on saying that magic was really, really dangerous, but some people just won't listen – especially witches!' He jumped down off the rag pile and glanced around disapprovingly. 'Well, there's no point in staying in this dump any longer! I'll have to go out into the great, wide world and seek my fortune!'

And since there was nothing to eat in the larder, he set off straight away.

CHAPTER TWO

A Lot to Learn

Wickedoz had looked down on a lot of the world from the front of Tottie Gribble's broomstick. He soon discovered, however, that zooming over the ground on nights of the full moon was a very different thing from walking upon it. In fact, the world seemed a far greater and wider place than he had thought and he had no idea of what direction to take to find his fortune. Wherever it lay, he hoped it would be in a place where there was food, because he was getting peckish.

It took the rest of the afternoon to descend the mountain and by the time Wickedoz reached the narrow path that led off down the valley below it, the sun was setting red and purple.

'There must be a village somewhere along

this path,' Wickedoz said to himself. 'With my good looks and a bit of charm, there won't be any trouble getting myself some food and a place to stay the night.'

The path joined a wide road then ran into a hamlet of thatched cottages. In the garden of the first cottage, a kind-faced elderly lady was taking washing off a line. Her mouth was filled with wooden pegs. Wickedoz nudged the garden gate open and sat down with his tail curled around his paws, trying his best to look handsome.

When the lady finally noticed Wickedoz, she gave a cry of surprise that scattered her pegs everywhere.

'Goodness gracious, puss, you fair gave me a turn!' she warbled. 'My, but you're a fine cat, to be sure! I haven't seen you around these parts before. Where have you sprung from, I wonder?'

'Up the mountain, actually,' Wickedoz replied chattily. 'I used to belong to Tottie Gribble, but I'm afraid she's had an unfortunate accident. I was just wondering if I might trouble you for . . .'

When Wickedoz first started speaking, the old lady frowned, then she went pale and finally she fainted. Her legs buckled under her and she fell face down on her front lawn with a soft thud.

'Well, well!' said Wickedoz, puzzled. 'I wonder what caused that?'

A cart came rattling down the road, driven by a sleepy-looking farmer.

'I say there!' Wickedoz called out to him. 'The old woman in this cottage appears to have had some sort of funny turn. Do you think you might . . .'

The farmer's eyes bulged, he gave a hoarse scream and flicked the reins to set his horse and cart careering on up the road.

'What on earth is the matter with everybody?' Wickedoz said aloud.

'You are!' a cheeky voice replied.

Wickedoz looked up and saw a robin peering down at him from a thatched roof. 'Me?' he said. 'What's wrong with me?'

'You can talk,' said the robin.

'So can you!'

'Ah, but you can talk human talk,' the robin explained. 'People don't like that.'

Wickedoz felt very confused and scratched inside his left ear to see if it would help.

'If people don't like human talk, why do *they* do it?' he asked.

'They don't mind when they do it *themselves*,' the robin said. 'It's when animals do it that they go a bit peculiar.'

'What a nuisance!' Wickedoz fretted. 'How am I going to get something to eat if I can't tell anybody how hungry I am?'

'You could try hunting,' suggested the robin. 'All the cats I've ever met love hunting.'

'And what do they hunt?'

'Mice, rats and . . . birds, mostly,' said the robin.

17

'How do they cook them?'

'They don't,' said the robin.

'You mean they eat them raw?' cried Wickedoz. 'That's the most disgusting thing I ever heard in my life!'

'You've got a lot to learn,' observed the robin, and flew away in case Wickedoz decided to learn about hunting birds.

CHAPTER THREE

Living on Wits

Wickedoz spent a miserable night under an oak tree in a field. The earth was hard and lumpy, which made a proper night's sleep impossible. Whenever Wickedoz managed to doze off, he dreamed about food. That made his empty stomach gurgle and the noise woke him up. By the time the sky was grey with dawn, Wickedoz was more tired and hungry than he had ever been in his life. To make matters worse, the people in the hamlet were early risers and were already up and about cooking breakfast. Wonderful dribble-making smells reached Wickedoz's nose and made it twitch.

'I can't go on!' Wickedoz groaned. 'Starving to death is no way of seeking my fortune! I'll have to go on the scrounge.'

After a quick wash, to make sure his coat

was gleaming, Wickedoz left the field and went padding off into the hamlet. He came to a cottage whose front window was open. Inside he could see a plump man and woman about to sit down to a sumptuous breakfast. There were fried eggs, thick rashers of ham and golden-brown kippers all sizzling and steaming and filling the air with a fragrance that drove Wickedoz half-wild.

'What a fine spread, Aggie m'dear!' drooled the man.

'Ah, John. You'm right there!' the woman sighed contentedly.

'It looks almost too good to eat,' said the man. 'Almost,' he added, steering his pot belly under the table, 'but not quite!'

Wickedoz thought quickly. If talking didn't work, perhaps playing dumb would. He cleared his throat and, feeling incredibly stupid, said, 'Um . . . *miaow?*'

'Did you say something, Aggie m'dear?' asked the man.

'Not a word, John.'

'*Miaow!*' said Wickedoz loudly. '*Miaow, miaow*, purr, purr!'

The man's podgy and curious face appeared at the window. When he caught sight of Wickedoz he blinked hard.

'Why . . . 'tis a cat, Aggie,' he informed his wife.

'*Miaow!*' Wickedoz called urgently. '*Miaow!*'

'Why,' murmured the man, ''tis almost like the cat were trying to tell me something.' A frown appeared on his forehead. It made the top of his face look like crinkly cooking fat.

'*MIAOW!*' roared Wickedoz. '*MI* – oh, what's the use! Of course I'm trying to tell you

21

something! I'm starving hungry, you great fool!'

The man's face went the colour of buttercups and then the colour of used dishwater. 'Aggie!' he quailed. 'The c-cat spoke to me! It spoke!'

'Spoke, John?' said the woman. 'But it can't have, m'dear! You look quite ill. It's back to bed with you. You lie down quiet and I'll brew you a crock o' dandelion tea.'

Before Wickedoz's delighted eyes, the plump woman took the plump man by the arm and led him away. As quick as a thought, Wickedoz was in through the window and up on the table. He ate two rashers of ham, lapped the yolks out of four eggs in as much time as it takes to tell, seized a kipper from a warming dish and sprang straight from the table out of the window. He ran as fast as he could, considering the extra weight he was carrying inside and outside.

'Now some would call that stealing,' Wickedoz told himself, 'but I call it living on my wits. It's the only way a talking ex-witch's cat *can* live!'

CHAPTER FOUR

Snarl

When Wickedoz had found a safe hiding place inside a hedge, he curled up next to his kipper. 'There's nothing a cat likes better than a quick snooze after a slap-up feed,' he said as he fell asleep. And when he woke, he found that there was nothing like sleep for giving a cat an appetite, so he ate the kipper before starting off once more to seek his fortune.

The morning sun was bright and warm. Wickedoz made easy progress along the road, but whenever he heard the rattling of a cart or the clopping of a horse's hooves, he quickly hid in case he was being pursued for his theft.

Just before mid-day, Wickedoz reached the end of the valley. Before him stretched a thick forest. In the far distance gleamed a pinkish mountain. There was no sign of any town or

villages or farms.

'Oh, dear!' said Wickedoz miserably. 'Looks like I won't be doing much scrounging for a while.'

Despite his doubts, when Wickedoz entered the forest a peculiar tingle of excitement ran through the tip of his tail. It made him think that he was somehow a little nearer to finding his fortune.

Overhead, the birds were singing busily in the trees – though it didn't sound like singing to Wickedoz because he could understand what they were saying.

'Push off!' a thrush bawled at a neighbour. 'This is my place! I've been raising families here for years! You come one hop nearer and I'll bop you one on the beak!'

'Oh yeah?' sneered the neighbour. 'Like to see you try, bird-brain!'

Squirrels, startled by Wickedoz's approach, yelled out, 'Cat alert! Cat alert! Scatter!' and scampered up into the shelter of the trees. In the undergrowth, rabbits whispered nervously.

'Has he gone yet, Fluff?'

'He's still there, Lugs! He looks a real brute!'

A little further on, Wickedoz overheard a pair of hedgehogs feeding.

'I've said it before and I'll say it again,' one declared in a slurpy sort of voice, 'for grand eating, you just can't beat a fat, juicy slug!'

The other hedgehog agreed by burping loudly.

'Ah!' Wickedoz sighed. 'Nature! So quiet! So peaceful!'

Apart from the noise, the journey was uneventful. One part of the forest looked very much like the next part and one tree looked very much like all the other trees to Wickedoz.

'This is getting tedious!' said Wickedoz. 'I

thought seeking one's fortune was supposed to be an adventure!'

It was not long before Wickedoz regretted his words. He came to a pool fed by a bubbling spring and as he was taking a long drink from it, he felt eyes watching him. At first, Wickedoz thought it might be a rabbit, waiting for him to leave before it took a drink itself – but then the feeling changed. Wickedoz suddenly knew that he was in great danger. His muscles tensed. His ears flicked this way and that, listening carefully and he dabbed at the air with his nose for clues. He caught a trace of a smell that made him want to sneeze.

'Gad, what a disgusting niff!' he exclaimed. 'Whatever can . . .' His voice died away to a dry squeak as an enormous wild cat poured itself down a nearby tree trunk and advanced on him. The cat was at least three times the size of Wickedoz and had eyes like green bonfires. Its long fangs hung down over its bottom lip like white needles. It did not look friendly and the thick rope of its tail lashed from side to side.

'Come on, wits!' Wickedoz urged. 'Think of something!'

The wild cat muttered to itself in a voice like distant thunder.

'First, I'm gonna claw his face! Then, after I've chewed off one of his ears and spat it out I'm gonna – '

'Hello there!' Wickedoz called cheerily.

The wild cat's stride faltered. Forest animals usually ran away from it. Being greeted was not something it was used to.

'Glorious day, isn't it?' said Wickedoz. 'I'm Wickedoz and you're . . . er?'

'I'm Snarl,' growled the cat. It came to a halt and sniffed suspiciously. 'What kind of cat are you?'

'I'm an ex-witch's cat,' said Wickedoz.

'What's an ex-witch?'

'It would take too long to explain,' answered Wickedoz. 'And, er, you're a wild cat, right?'

'Right!' said Snarl.

'And you live right here in the forest?'

'Yeah!' said Snarl.

'Dear, dear!' tutted Wickedoz. 'Tell me, does it get cold in winter?'

'It freezes up solid!' Snarl shivered at the memory.

'And do you catch cold at all?' enquired Wickedoz.

'Nah!' shrugged Snarl.

'No coughs, shivers, headaches, ringing in the ears, anything like that?'

'Nah!'

'Good!' Wickedoz declared. 'Well, Mr Snarl, there doesn't appear to be a great deal the matter with you. Just carry on as you are, plenty of exercise and a healthy diet and you should be fine!'

'Oh,' said Snarl. 'Right! Er, well, thanks for letting me know.'

'Any time,' purred Wickedoz. 'And now, if you'll excuse me, I do have other animals to see.'

'Of course,' Snarl said sympathetically. 'Don't let me keep you.'

Wickedoz swished his tail in a salute and walked away as steadily as he could.

'Whew! There's more to seeking my fortune than I bargained for!' he told himself. 'Now I've had an adventure, I'm not sure that I don't prefer the tedious bits!'

CHAPTER FIVE

Bold Outlaws

After the shock and relief of his narrow escape from Snarl had worn off, Wickedoz noticed that he was hungry. The forest shadows were deepening into the evening and the chances of finding a cottage where he could scrounge food before nightfall were growing slim.

'Looks like another restless, hungry night,' he said grimly – but just as he said it, he heard a sound that made his eyes go narrow and mysterious. It was the sound of someone singing. Wickedoz followed the voice, taking care to be as quiet as possible.

'Alas, alack and rue the day,' went the song,
'Alas the night-time too,
Woe in the dawn and evening,
Hey nonny, nonny noo!'

There was a clearing in the forest. In the centre of the clearing stood a handsome young man, clad in velvet, strumming a lute and singing. His pale hands and face glimmered in the dusky air. Seated around the young man were three others whose faces did not glimmer – they were far too grimy. There was a long, lanky man with a face like a worn hatchet, a round man with a round face and a short man wearing wire-framed spectacles with thick lenses. They were variously snivelling, sobbing and wiping their noses on their sleeves as the young man continued singing. All this Wickedoz noticed at a glance, but even more importantly he noticed the iron pot heating up over a fire outside a large tent.

'Scroungy time!' growled Wickedoz.

'Alas the sky, alack the moon,' sang the young man,
'How sad the stars and sun!
O, woe to me and woe to thee
And woe to everyone!'

The song ended in a loud, tragic chord on the lute. The audience, too upset to applaud, took a minute or two to pull itself together.

'I just can't 'elp it,' the short, bespectacled man said tearfully. 'I do love a good dirge!'

'I'm of your opinion on that matter, Ned,' said the lanky man, wiping tears from his eyes and flicking them on to the ground.

'Aye!' the round man agreed hoarsely. 'Give me a song about weepin', wailin' and misery with a catchy tune so I can sing along!'

Wickedoz kept one ear on the conversation as he crept around the clearing towards the cooking pot. The enticing smell of stewing mutton drew him on. He got closer and closer . . . and then a careless whisk of his tail rustled some dry bracken-fronds.

The young man with the lute turned

sharply, his eyes alarmed. 'Who's there?' he quailed.

The other three jumped to their feet. The round man picked up a rusty pike and held it so that it wavered about all over the place. The lanky man drew a rust-spotted sword whose end was slightly bent and held it out at arm's length. The bespectacled man, facing in entirely the wrong direction, struggled to notch an arrow on to the string of a rather mildewed bow.

'Come on,' trembled the young man. 'Show yourself!'

Wickedoz had no choice but to trust his luck. He came out from cover and walked into plain view. The men all sagged with relief.

'Why, 'tis only a cat!' laughed the round man. 'And there we were, frightened of a plain, ordinary ol' moggie!'

'Well, to be perfectly honest with you,' Wickedoz confessed, 'I'm not exactly what you might call an ordinary cat. I thought I'd explain that straight away to avoid any misunderstanding later on. So, the fact of the matter is, I'm a very extraordinary cat, I'm absolutely ravenous and my only hope of getting a meal is if you share yours with me. Now, what do you say to that?'

There were knocking knees and loud gulps. All the men looked terrified – except the young man in velvet. He had a puzzled frown on his face. 'Hang on, chaps!' he said. 'There's something strange here! Tell me if I'm wrong, but cats don't *usually* talk, do they?'

'Cat?' mumbled the bespectacled man. 'I've never seen a cat like it! One 'uge, thick, brown leg and covered all over in green fur!'

'Ned,' said the lanky man, 'that's a tree you're lookin' at. The cat's over there!'

'They do say,' the round man rasped as the pike trembled in his hands, 'that evil spirits can take the form of black cats to lure poor mortals to their doom!'

'Who says?' snorted Wickedoz.

'Well . . .' faltered the round man. 'You know . . . folks.'

'Rubbish!' exclaimed Wickedoz. 'Look, either use those weapons to finish me off or let me share your supper.'

There was a muttered conference, then the bespectacled man said, 'You're welcome to share our supper on account of 'ow 'tis only friendly what with you bein' so 'ungry. Also, if we chopped you up, 'twould likely be a bit on the messy side and it might put us off our grub.'

37

'Great!' cried Wickedoz. 'I'm Wickedoz. I'm an ex-witch's cat. I'm seeking my fortune and I live by using my wits.'

'I'm Ned O'Lantern,' said the bespectacled man. 'Master bowman and bold outlaw!'

'And my name,' said the lanky man with the sword, 'is Seth Green. I'm a fencin' fury and bold outlaw!'

'Perkin Lumbold,' said the round man. 'I

prod a bit with the ol' pike and I'm an outlaw bold.'

Everyone looked expectantly at the young man in velvet, who appeared to be thinking about something else. When he noticed the eyes staring at him, he jumped. 'Oh, me? Sorry! Um, the name's Gerald Fitzgerald-Fitzgerald the Third. Oh, and I'm an outlaw, of course! Frightfully keen on it!'

'Now we all know each other, shall we eat?' said Wickedoz.

CHAPTER SIX

The Duke of Boldcombe

By the time Wickedoz and the outlaws had finished eating, evening had turned to night. A hush had fallen over the forest and the only sounds were the snapping of twigs in the fire and the hooting of owls far-off.

Now that he was able to think of something other than food, Wickedoz grew curious about his companions. They seemed a friendly bunch – far too friendly for outlaws, in fact. And then there was the way they had handled their weapons, almost as if they were frightened of them themselves. Something was not quite right.

Most curiously of all, whenever Wickedoz looked at Gerald, his tail tingled in a fortune-finding way.

'Tell me,' he said casually. 'How's business in

the outlaw trade?'

There was much coughing and umming and head-scratching at this.

'It's a job to say, really,' said Ned, chewing his bottom lip.

'We 'aven't been outlaws all that long,' admitted Seth.

'How long?' asked Wickedoz.

'About three weeks,' blushed Seth.

'Two weeks, five days and thirteen hours!' groaned Perkin, consulting a large pocket watch.

'I see!' said Wickedoz. 'And what did you do before you became outlaws?'

'I was 'ead gardener to the Duke of Boldcombe!' Ned said proudly. 'My sweet peas used to win silver cups!'

'I was the Duke of Boldcombe's official window cleaner!' said Seth. 'The windows of Boldcombe Manor used to glitter like jewels!'

'I was chief washer-up in the Duke of Boldcombe's kitchen,' said Perkin. 'I washed plates until they were clean enough to eat your dinner off!'

Everyone gazed expectantly at Gerald, who looked miles away.

'Oh, me?' he giggled nervously. 'I used to be the Duke of Boldcombe.'

The tingling in Wickedoz's tail was now so strong that he had to wave it about. 'What happened?'

Gerald's face grew pained. 'It was the strangest thing!' he said glumly. 'I was on my way home from a state visit. Top-hole do, you know, so I was wearing my best togs and had all my men-at-arms with me. Anyway, my horse happened to squash a newt. Accident, of course! Well, all of a sudden this old crone

pops out from nowhere and starts ranting and raving. Seems the newt was some sort of pet of hers, named Anthony. The next thing I knew, there was a flash of light and my own men-at-arms were putting me in chains! They took me back to Boldcombe Manor and locked me up.'

'Terrible, it was!' growled Ned. 'That old woman just took over. The men-at-arms did everythin' she told 'em to do. They ripped all the flowers out of the garden and planted nightshade and 'enbane instead!'

'And she turned all the windows black 'cos she didn't want folks seein' in!' burst out Seth.

'And she eats out of wooden bowls!' wailed Perkin. 'She smashed all the china in a fit of rage!'

'Well, in the end we couldn't stand it no more!' said Ned. 'In the dead of night, we managed to free 'is grace, the Duke and we ran away.'

'Ah!' nodded Seth. 'And 'tis said the old woman 'as sworn to take a terrible revenge on us all!'

'And if she ever catches us . . .' whimpered Perkin.

'I hate to think what Mistress Moonwater would do to us!' sighed Gerald.

'Mistress Moonwater!' cried Wickedoz. 'But she's a notorious witch!'

Wickedoz was so excited that night he couldn't go to sleep for the plans and ideas that were sizzling away like fireworks in his head. The outlaws were taking it in turns to keep watch. When it was Gerald's turn, Wickedoz sidled up to him and spoke in a low voice. 'Gerald, how would you fancy being Duke of Boldcombe again?'

'Now you come to mention it, I think it would be quite jolly,' said Gerald.

'I think I have a plan that would put you back in your rightful place in Boldcombe Manor,' whispered Wickedoz.

'But what about Mistress Moonwater?'

'You leave Mistress Moonwater to me,' Wickedoz said confidently. 'I know a bit about witches!'

'Tell me,' frowned Gerald, 'this plan of yours . . . would there be any risk involved?'

'If it went wrong, the witch would almost certainly do such terrible things to us that it would turn your hair white if I told you,' Wickedoz said gravely.

'Golly!' gulped Gerald. 'You'd better tell me about the plan instead!'

Wickedoz did – and in the morning he had to tell it all again to Ned, Seth and Perkin.

CHAPTER SEVEN

Mistress Moonwater Rules OK

While all this was going on, over in Boldcombe Manor Mistress Moonwater was having a great time. As soon as she had installed herself in the manor house, she issued a proclamation saying that every day was her birthday and that everybody in the duchy had to send her presents. She sent men-at-arms (who had been enchanted) to collect the presents. Anyone who complained was cursed with boils on the bottom and the brave few who refused to give any presents at all were turned into sheep.

'I can't deny I'm nasty!' chuckled Mistress Moonwater as the servants laid the dining-hall table for breakfast. She reached into her robes and brought out a pocket-sized magic mirror. Mistress Moonwater simpered at her own reflection. 'Mirror, mirror in my hand,' she chanted coyly, 'who's the worst in all the land?'

'You are,' said the mirror. 'No contest!'

'Crikey!' beamed Mistress Moonwater.

'There's no doubt about it,' went on the magic mirror. 'You are the nastiest, most despicable witch ever. When they draw up the list of the foulest, ugliest, gummiest old bats, your name will be right up there at the top!'

'Lumme!' sighed Mistress Moonwater.

'And as well as being the meanest and most cantankerous witch this century,' the mirror

confided, 'there's also your smell to be taken into consideration.'

'My smell?' Mistress Moonwater cried, clapping her hands with glee.

'Your breath could knock down an elephant at twenty metres,' announced the mirror.

'Enough, enough!' exclaimed Mistress Moonwater, replacing the mirror in her robes. 'I'm so wonderfully wicked that it's almost embarrassing!' She was so thrilled, that when the servants entered with her breakfast, she poured a jug of drinking chocolate over them. 'Don't say I never give you anything!' she cackled as they ran, screaming from the hall.

Witches, as is widely known, enjoy a large breakfast and Mistress Moonwater was no exception. She had cereals, bacon, toast and marmalade followed by steak, egg and chips and fried Christmas pudding, all washed down with mugs of steaming tea. As she chomped and slurped her way through the enormous meal, Mistress Moonwater read the begging letters that messengers had brought her from all over the duchy. They were mostly from people with boils on their bottoms or from the families of those she had turned into sheep. When Mistress Moonwater read the piteous accounts of children crying themselves to sleep for lack of their fathers, or begging in the streets because they had lost both parents, she laughed until her eyes streamed with tears.

'Marvellous, marvellous!' she crowed as she finished the last letter and flung it over her shoulder. 'What a super start to the day! It's put me in the mood to do something mega-bad!'

She snapped her fingers. There was a loud 'FLUMP!' and a trumpet appeared in her hands. The witch raised the trumpet to her lips and played the post-horn gallop that was a call to her men at arms. The tramp-tramp-tramp of marching feet sounded from the courtyard and Mistress Moonwater threw open the black window to look.

The men-at-arms were lined up in neat ranks, standing stiffly to attention. Their pale faces and blank eyes showed how strongly they were enchanted – they were no more than puppets for Mistress Moonwater to use as she chose.

'Attention, my merry men!' screeched the witch. 'I want the first four rows of you to go hither through the land and the next four rows to go thither. I want you to seek out all the children with red hair and freckles and throw them into duck-ponds. And make sure the

ponds have got plenty of that slimy green stuff floating about in them!'

'We hear and obey!' the men-at-arms chanted tonelessly. The first eight rows broke into a jog-trot and left the courtyard through the main gate.

'Stay there, the rest of you,' commanded Mistress Moonwater. 'You are to guard my precious person!'

'We hear and obey!' replied the men.

Mistress Moonwater closed the window, her shoulders shaking with mirth. 'And tomorrow, it'll be the turn of left-handed people with curly hair!' she promised herself.

Just at that moment, a servant entered the dining hall, trembling with fear. His hair was caked in dried drinking chocolate.

'You fool!' scowled Mistress Moonwater. 'Can't you see I'm gloating? Don't you know better than to interrupt a witch in mid-gloat?'

'B-beg pardon, your h-hagitude,' mumbled the servant. 'B-but someone wishes to see you so urgently he says he won't take no for an answer! He says he simply can't wait!'

'Pah!' fumed Mistress Moonwater. 'Who is this idiot?'

'P-please, your malevolence, it's the old Duke – I mean, the young Duke – I mean, the bloke who used to be the Duke!'

'You gibbering wretch!' roared the witch. 'Not even Gerald Fitzgerald-Fitzgerald the Third would be stupid enough to return here when he knows what I might do to him!'

Suddenly, Gerald's voice came drifting through the dining hall's open door. 'I come on wings of love!'

'I've underestimated that young man,' Mistress Moonwater said softly. 'He's a bigger nincompoop than I thought!'

CHAPTER EIGHT

Wickedoz the Traitor

Gerald appeared in the doorway. His face was stretched into a soupy smile. He strummed a chord on his lute. Behind him came Ned, Seth and Perkin. They were pushing a trolley on which was a large wooden crate with air-holes in the side, tied up in a pink ribbon bow.

'Darling!' cried Gerald.

Mistress Moonwater looked behind her. There was no one there. Puzzled, she looked under the dining table but there was no one there either.

'Darling!' Gerald cried again.

'Who me?' snapped Mistress Moonwater.

'Who else . . . angel?' cooed Gerald.

'Get off, you great wet nelly!' hissed Mistress Moonwater. 'Being on the run has turned your brain into rhubarb yoghurt!'

'Mock not!' insisted Gerald, dropping on to one knee and strumming a dramatic chord. 'Every day and every night of my lonely banishment in the deep dark forest, the memory of your face has haunted me. I've tried to keep away, but it's no use. I've come to ask for your hand!'

'My hand?' frowned Mistress Moonwater. 'What do you want to do with my hand?'

'I mean, I want to marry you!' gushed Gerald.

'Marry me?' shouted Mistress Moonwater. 'Yeuk! I'm a witch! Witches don't get married because they're wedded to the Black Arts! Marriage is all soppy, kissy-kissy stuff!'

'You little heart-breaker!' sighed Gerald.

'Besides, you're not my type!' added Mistress Moonwater. 'Now then, how would you like to meet your end, dearie? Ripped to pieces by giant land-crabs? Drained dry by vampire bats? Or how about something simple but classic, like boiling in oil?'

'The present!' Ned whispered urgently. 'Tell her about the present!'

'Er, oh yes, of course!' said Gerald, snapping his fingers. 'To show you my undying devotion and never-ending love and all that sort of thing, I've brought you a present.'

'A pressie?' warbled Mistress Moonwater, her eyes glowing with greed. 'For me? What an absolutely all-right thing to do!'

'I'm sure you'll like it,' said Gerald.

Mistress Moonwater tripped lightly across the dining hall, pulled at the bow and the sides of the crate folded neatly back to reveal Wickedoz. His coat shone like wet paint and he had put on his most mysterious, most magic slit-eyed look.

'Ooh!' declared Mistress Moonwater.

'You're a fine figure of a feline, aren't you?'

'I'm glad you think so,' Wickedoz said. 'I'm not just a pretty face, though. I'm a dab-hand at assisting with the old spells and I'm much more presentable in polite society than a newt!'

'S-o-o-o!' drawled Mistress Moonwater. 'You know something about magic?'

'I'm an ex-witch's cat,' Wickedoz explained. 'Temporarily out of work. Only one careful owner, who disintegrated in an unfortunate accident.'

'Ha!' laughed Mistress Moonwater. 'So you're looking for a witch to assist and I'm looking for a new witch's assistant! Fancy working with me?'

'Righty-ho!' cried Wickedoz. 'But what about this lot?'

He flicked his tail to indicate Gerald and the others.

Mistress Moonwater flung open the window and called out, 'Ten of you lot, up here right away!'

'To hear is to obey!' came the reply.

'What do you think should be done with them?' the witch asked Wickedoz.

'Well, they did bring me here and they took good care of me on the way,' said Wickedoz. 'They went without food themselves so that I could be fed. They pandered to my every whim and were always kind, considerate and polite. What say we lock them in a dark, spidery cellar and deal with them later?'

'Capital!' shrieked Mistress Moonwater. 'I like your style! You're almost as treacherous as I am!' She turned as the ten men-at-arms marched into the hall. 'Take these miserable creatures down to the cellars and lock them up at once!'

'To hear is to obey!' chorused the men.

As he was dragged from the hall, Gerald called out, 'You traitor, Wickedoz! I think you're a thoroughly bad sort!'

Wickedoz and Mistress Moonwater looked at one another and burst into peals of merry, malicious laughter.

CHAPTER NINE

Spells and Shelves

Witches, as is widely known, enjoy a large luncheon and Mistress Moonwater was not one to stint herself. Wickedoz was given a bowl of liver, cooked to perfection, while Mistress Moonwater feasted on slices of ox, a turkey and a suckling pig.

As she munched and crunched her way through lunch, Mistress Moonwater entertained herself by discussing with Wickedoz the fate of the unfortunate Duke and his faithful servants.

'Something spectacular . . .' mused the witch. 'Something that will be a talking point among the other witches . . .'

'Turn them into sheep,' suggested Wickedoz.

'No,' said Mistress Moonwater. 'I'm tired of

sheep. I've been doing a lot of sheep just lately.'

'How about summoning up a few thousand snakes?' said Wickedoz.

'Too noisy!' complained Mistress Moonwater. 'There'll be so much hissing and screaming that I'll get a headache!'

'How about turning them into toads?' asked Wickedoz.

'Too corny!'

'Ordeal by demon?'

'Too vulgar!' said Mistress Moonwater distastefully.

Wickedoz thought hard for a moment, then

flounced his tail in excited triumph. 'Got it!' he exclaimed. 'It's new, it's clever and it gets our partnership off to a perfect start!'

'Oh, do tell!' chortled Mistress Moonwater. 'I love it to bits already and I don't even know what it is!'

'Turn them into mice!' announced Wickedoz. 'And then, when they're mice, I'll hunt them down!'

Mistress Moonwater whooped with delight, slapped her thighs and drummed her feet on the floor. 'You are a one, Wickedoz! The other witches will be green when they find out!'

'Just think of it as being the first step on a long journey of really low-down dirty tricks!' purred Wickedoz.

'We'll do it this very afternoon!' Mistress Moonwater proclaimed. 'Then we'll have the sort of big dinner that witches enjoy. What would you say to a roasted swan, Wickedoz?'

'Nothing,' retorted Wickedoz. 'I'd just eat it!'

When lunch had been cleared away, Mistress Moonwater ordered the prisoners to be brought in. They looked miserable and fearful and their iron fetters clanked.

'This is all your fault, Wickedoz!' cried Ned. 'I knew we should never 'ave trusted you!'

'An evil spirit come to lure us to our doom!' droned Perkin. 'Just like I said!'

'Silence!' shouted Mistress Moonwater. 'Cringe, fools, as I prepare for ... Black Magic!' As she spoke, she pressed a secret button at the side of the marble mantelpiece. A section of the wall slid back to reveal a secret chamber, packed with books, scrolls, charts and shelf upon shelf of magical paraphernalia.

'Most impressive!' Wickedoz commented.

'Isn't it?' agreed Mistress Moonwater. 'Ooh, I do love feeling smug!'

She set to work at once. She set a cauldron of water over the fire, and as it was coming to the boil, she consulted a book of spells. While she was gathering the ingredients for the magic together, Wickedoz noticed how shaky the shelves were. In fact, the whole shelf unit was so rickety that it was a wonder it could stand at all.

'Perfect!' he whispered.

'What's perfect?' demanded Mistress Moonwater.

'I mean, it's a perfect day for this sort of thing!' Wickedoz replied quickly.

'Hush!' urged Mistress Moonwater. 'This is no time for chit-chat! The spell is a tricky one and I need to concentrate.'

She dropped one ingredient after another into the cauldron, muttering spells under her breath and making signs with her hands. The cauldron's contents glowed yellow, then green, then blue.

Behind her in the chamber, Wickedoz crouched. He tensed his muscles and a shining ripple ran up his back. It would have to be the highest jump he had ever made and he was only going to get one chance at it.

'By Hecate and Astarte . . .' muttered Mistress Moonwater. The cauldron glowed purple and Wickedoz knew if he left it a moment longer it would be too late.

He sprang. He pushed with his back legs and went soaring into the air. At the top of his jump, he twisted around and kicked the top of the shelf unit as hard as he could. It rocked, bottles and flasks clinking together and then it toppled.

Mistress Moonwater turned to see the shelf unit falling on top of her and she screamed.

There was a mighty crash. Lotions and salves and charms and essences all mixed together and started to fizz. A crackling explosion accompanied a bolt of pink lightning and there was a great deal of rolling green smoke. When the smoke cleared, there was

nothing left of Mistress Moonwater but a greasy mark on the floor.

Wickedoz squeezed out from under a dried crocodile. His fur was a little rumpled, but he was otherwise unharmed.

'Well done, Wickedoz!' called Gerald. 'Absolutely first-rate show! Your plan worked a treat!'

'It did, didn't it?' said Wickedoz. 'It worked like magic!'

CHAPTER TEN

Fortune

All over the duchy, the spells of Mistress Moonwater were broken. Boils vanished and bewildered-looking people suddenly appeared among flocks of sheep, their mouths filled with half-chewed grass. Men-at-arms found themselves at the sides of duck-ponds that were filled with slimy and unhappy red-haired freckled children.

It took ages to put everything right. Gerald answered hundreds of begging letters and sent roomfuls of presents back to the people who had sent them. His chief assistants as he set about these awesome tasks were Ned, Seth, Perkin and Wickedoz. Wickedoz was actually a great help and came up with all sorts of clever ideas.

At last, it was all done. Gerald celebrated

with a large banquet at which Wickedoz was the guest of honour.

Towards the end of the festivities, Gerald noticed that Wickedoz had left his place and went to look for him. He discovered the cat outside on the terrace, gazing up at an autumn moon that was the colour of cheese.

'What ho, Wickedoz, old chap!' Gerald greeted him. 'Penny for your thoughts and all that sort of thing.'

'To be honest with you, Gerald, I'm feeling restless,' Wickedoz confessed. 'I know I ought to be content and know when I'm well off, but after Tottie Gribble had her accident, I set off to seek my fortune.'

'And you found it!' exclaimed Gerald. 'Here, at Boldcombe Manor.'

'I don't know!' sighed Wickedoz. 'You see, just these last few days my tail has been tingling like anything!'

'Ah!' said Gerald. 'And that means you'll be travelling on, I suppose?'

'Yes. It's about time I was going,' replied Wickedoz.

'But, I say, Wickedoz, how will you manage without food or money and all that?' demanded Gerald.

'Me?' said Wickedoz. 'I'll live on my wits!'

And he stepped off the terrace and vanished into the soft autumn dark.

Also by Andrew Matthews

DIXIE'S DEMON

When your pet is small and a bit on the fiendish side, Dixie discovers, you get an *awful* lot of hassle. You get into trouble with your parents, your friends laugh at you and the biggest yobbo in school wants to duff you up. Added to which, demons have some . . . well . . . *peculiar* personal habits.

A very funny story of one boy and his demon.

Andrew Matthews

DR MONSOON TAGGERT'S AMAZING FINISHING ACADEMY

'My dear Arabella,' the letter read, 'I can tell you're not very happy. If you come to my Academy, I'll try to put things right for you. I don't promise that I'll succeed, mind you, but I do promise to try my best. Yours sincerely, Monsoon Taggert (Dr)'

Dr Taggert's magic has begun . . . Arabella's quest takes her on a helter-skelter, snakes and ladders adventure until her wish comes true.

This hilarious tale was shortlisted for the Smarties Award.

Andrew Matthews

MISTRESS MOONWATER

Mistress Moonwater, the most chronic chrone in the chronicle, is living in semi-retirement in Dunspellin Castle. Meanwhile, in Heartland, a fairy tale is in the making. Princess Cheryl, the beloved and nearly beautiful, is to marry Prince Craig of Constantia, the quite clever prince. Or is she?

Egged on by Lord Cringe of Nobbly Wallop, Mistress Moonwater has other ideas . . .

Andrew Matthews

MONSTER HULLABALOO!

When Mr Monster meets Mrs Monster he is
thrilled to bits – he won't have to be lonely any
more. So you can just imagine how happy he
is when Baby Monster arrives. And when
Granny Monster comes to stay, there's a real
Monster Hullabaloo . . .

Andrew Matthews

THE QUIET PIRATE

'Yo ho ho and a cup of tea. A pirate's life is not for me!'

William Barrett counts all the peas in the Kingdom of Dunroamin. He is quite happy until his swashbuckling uncle whisks him away one day to turn him into a pirate. Before long, William and his cat are mixed up with a cowardly Duke, a stubborn Princess and the barmiest crew of bungling pirates ever to sail the Seven Seas!

Andrew Matthews

S. CLAUS – THE TRUTH!

So you want to know the truth about S. Claus? Well let me just say a certain reindeer isn't too happy with his job. No one told him he'd be working one day a year for a living! Read all about it . . .

A collection of six deliciously funny festive tales!

Andrew Matthews

WOLF PIE

What happens when a cruel and greedy King and Queen order a dish they've never eaten before? Who ends up in a barrel of jellyfish? Why do the Apprentice Chefs run away? And what have wolves got to do with it?

If your taste is for stories which are funny (and a bit rude!) open up this pie and discover its very strange contents . . .

W. J. Corbett

DEAR GRUMBLE

When Tom and Clare Price hear the sound of hooves clip-clopping up the lane and the familiar cry of 'Any old rags?' they are ready to swap their old woollens for the rag-and-bone man's goldfish. But then they see something 'a little larger' tied to the back of the cart – something so special that spoilt Felicity wants it too . . . The race is on . . .

". . . full of delightful eccentricities and jokes – the manner is sublime."   *Robert Westall*

A selected list of titles available from Mammoth

While every effort is made to keep prices low, it is sometimes necessary to increase prices at short notice. Mandarin Paperbacks reserves the right to show new retail prices on covers which may differ from those previously advertised in the text or elsewhere.

The prices shown below were correct at the time of going to press.

☐	7497 0366 0	**Dilly the Dinosaur**	Tony Bradman	£2.50
☐	7497 0137 4	**Flat Stanley**	Jeff Brown	£2.50
☐	7497 0306 7	**The Chocolate Touch**	P Skene Catling	£2.50
☐	7497 0568 X	**Dorrie and the Goblin**	Patricia Coombs	£2.50
☐	7497 0114 5	**Dear Grumble**	W J Corbett	£2.50
☐	7497 0054 8	**My Naughty Little Sister**	Dorothy Edwards	£2.50
☐	7497 0723 2	**The Little Prince (colour ed.)**	A Saint-Exupery	£3.99
☐	7497 0305 9	**Bill's New Frock**	Anne Fine	£2.99
☐	7497 0590 6	**Wild Robert**	Diana Wynne Jones	£2.50
☐	7497 0661 9	**The Six Bullerby Children**	Astrid Lindgren	£2.50
☐	7497 0319 9	**Dr Monsoon Taggert's Amazing Finishing Academy**	Andrew Matthews	£2.50
☐	7497 0420 9	**I Don't Want To!**	Bel Mooney	£2.50
☐	7497 0833 6	**Melanie and the Night Animal**	Gillian Rubinstein	£2.50
☐	7497 0264 8	**Akimbo and the Elephants**	A McCall Smith	£2.50
☐	7497 0048 3	**Friends and Brothers**	Dick King-Smith	£2.50
☐	7497 0795 X	**Owl Who Was Afraid of the Dark**	Jill Tomlinson	£2.99

All these books are available at your bookshop or newsagent, or can be ordered direct from the publisher. Just tick the titles you want and fill in the form below.

Mandarin Paperbacks, Cash Sales Department, PO Box 11, Falmouth, Cornwall TR10 9EN.

Please send cheque or postal order, no currency, for purchase price quoted and allow the following for postage and packing:

UK including
BFPO
£1.00 for the first book, 50p for the second and 30p for each additional book ordered to a maximum charge of £3.00.

Overseas
including Eire
£2 for the first book, £1.00 for the second and 50p for each additional book thereafter.

NAME (Block letters) ....

ADDRESS ....

....

☐ I enclose my remittance for ....

☐ I wish to pay by Access/Visa Card Number ☐☐☐☐☐☐☐☐☐☐☐☐☐☐☐☐

Expiry Date ☐☐☐☐